THE BENEFITS
OF A BULLY

THE BENEFITS OF A BULLY

OF A BULLY

The Onyx Eyed Kids

L.A. Kendrick

ISBN   Paperback   978-1-956135-05-3
         eBook   978-1-956135-06-0

In memory of FANNIE MAE TRICE, June 29, 1908
Great Grandmother.

TABLE OF CONTENTS

INTRODUCTION

Well since the race has already begun, let me catch you good people up. See there is this race called "GYRO SHOT", it's for hand-eye coordination, athleticism, and on the move, cognitive thinking during fast-paced action. You have to run towards the starting line to activate the Gyro shoes, but you must reach at least six miles per hour before hitting the starting line or you are disqualified and your team has to compete without you. Once you reach that speed, I believe Mr. Brown said that it builds up kinetic energy that will give the nice kicks the ability to defy gravity. You know running up walls, across water, and all kinds of crazy stunts. The charge will last as long as you keep the shoes on and don't stay still over 30 seconds; I LOVE EM!

The objective of the game is to hit as many targets while moving through a maze and yep you guessed it with a slingshot; some targets are worth more than others. Kinda like the money ball in a basketball three point contest. At the end, whichever team has the most points wins, and I have been doing it big. Haven't lost yet, even though we did lose one kid who didn't practice much, he paid for that at the starting line, I've made up those lost points. This team is pretty tough though and they have this one kid giving us problems; we are in two teams of five... Well that was the game plan now it's four against five. We all have helmets, goggles, gloves, knee and elbow pads, you know for protection. This tough kid's hair is sticking out of his helmet from the back and sides, and I can't really see his face, but I will once we beat em. The track is like a water slide at an amusement park; some of the spaces are narrow some wide open. Boy you should see the kids bouncing off the walls, trying to keep up; OH I GOT IT, it's like Roller Derby that's a better picture for you. Forgive my manners I'm Sedale, Sedale Johnson and out here I take no prisoners; see you at the finish line!"

CHAPTER 1

They have traps set up all over the track, high-powered fans, barricades that pop outta nowhere. We've just lost two more on our team not too sure how many the other team has lost, but I just saw a kid blown right outta the arena as I dodged the surge of air from the fan. I couldn't help but laugh a little because the kid sounded like a hit dog as he was sent flying through the air. Right on call, here comes that kid with the hair jetting out of the helmet; the last couple of targets keep popping up and down. Haven't missed any targets yet, and this joker has not either I'm gonna run up the wall and get the next one.

"You ain't gonna beat me kid so just step off, and accept second place!" I yell out flipping over the next trap and firing my shot hitting the next to last target.

"Well cabbage head, tasting second place will be something you're just gonna have to get use, to because trust me I got this!" Hat hair kids says.

Whoa the kid just did the same move that I did, oh snap the final target is here just need to dodge the final obstacle. These shoes really let you get it; you can run up to thirty miles per hour that is so fast. This kid is my shadow, there it is and here is my final shot, BULLSEYE! Now for the roar of the crowd, wait a minute, the announcer just said it's a TIE, how!

"It is a tie, both team leaders hit the final mark simultaneously. This is a first in the history of the challenge!" The announcer says.

"Looks like you will be sharing the win catfish fin, only next time I will be standing alone with my team!" The helmet haired kid says.

The kid takes off the helmet and goggle's aww shoot it's a girl, a dirty cooty filled girl. This is so embarrassing; how in the world did we tie? I gotta have a good come back; she won't outrank or cap me.

"I knew from the poffy, puffs of your big ole pumpkin puffs that you where a girl!" I say. Oh man was that lame but that's all I got; hey she caught me off guard.

"Yeah whatever Sedale yeah, I know who you are; we go to the same school, I'm Turkeesha. Think fast chump stump and you should really work on your come backs!" Turkeesha replies.

She throws her helmet at me thinking that I wouldn't catch it, but I did real easy. Here comes the terrible twosome Sterling and Dexter.

"You can have this helmet back; it smells like sweaty socks and cigarettes!" I say.

"Man she's really good and pretty too; she gave you the business dog!" Sterling says.

"Yeah she was really good, we finished our challenges in Battle Bash and Think Fast. There was no ties with us; you must be slippin!" Dexter adds while laughing.

Whatever I say as Mr. Brown approaches us with a serious look on his face, which means only one thing, a NEW

ASSIGNMENT! We all go to attention as he meets us; he lets us know which room to go to get the briefing.

"You guys need to go and get cleaned up; we have a very serious issue that we need to brief you on. You have twenty minutes, make it happen!" Mr. Brown says as he takes off.

"Well Dexter, it might take a bit longer than twenty minutes to remove your kind of stink!" I say.

"I know you didn't, I'm clean, and what are you laughing at Sterling. With that peanut butter on your pants, or is it really peanut butter Donkey legs?" Dexter replies.

"Always thinking about food, that's why your pants are always tapping out!" Sterling says surprisingly with a good comeback.

Let's move fellas I say, we go to our rooms boy, do they have the best technology here? The shower is not a shower; let me break it down, you step in and it hits you with a blast of water that covers your body. Then you get to choose which smell you want, push the button, then it gets just a little bit bright, then just like that you are clean. I mean no germs, no dirt, and you stay fresh and so clean all day. Even your ears, nose, and fingernails are all clean. You step out totally dry; you still have to brush your teeth and put deodorant on, just so you don't rely on tech totally.

Time to get that briefing it seems pretty serious, I have learned a lot about the things that go bump in the night or hide under your bed or in closets. We all are getting pretty good, time for another challenge, let me find a seat...Oh ok got one the fellas have picked one for me.

"Has he started yet?" I ask because Mr. Brown has his back to us.

"Nope he's just standing there; people keep coming and going talking to him really low. Can't hear what they are saying!" Sterling responds.

Mr. Brown looks more intense than normal, it's like someone just stuck em in the butt with a needle and he refuses to yell. I always yell when I get stuck with needles, ok here we go now, the big assignment. The room is clearing of the other adults, and Mr. Brown walks in front of the viewscreen.

"Young people I hope you've been keeping up with your studies and training. This new mission will be challenging, as they all have, are and will be. In this image, you see that these look like normal everyday kids, some that you deal with at your old school. Now if you look closely, this is how they act with random adults, they simple walk up and act as if they are in distress, sitting in cars, in subways, leaving stores, parking lots. When they strike; some are really violent as they pounce, always in groups of three like a pack of wild dogs. They then drag their victims to undisclosed areas for some unknown purposes, key thing notice the eyes it is believed that they hypnotize their victims as their eyes emit this strange white light." Mr. Brown says.

"Dog they look really scary, I've seen them before or at least I think I have. Definitely in my nightmares!" Sterling replies in a low voice.

"Shut up dweeb, we need to hear this; you see everything in a nightmare buzzard belly!" Dexter says.

I gotta agree with Sterling on this one; these cats look creepy. I can't wait to hear the rest, get the gear and then get to work.

"There is a camping trip that is coming up, and it will be at one of the major national parks we've triangulated their origins to, so many people have been going missing without a trace for years. You will be taking a trip with volunteer adults, they don't know what is going on, and will need to be kept in the dark about it. You have to infiltrate and complete the mission and keep your secret identities intact. The trip will be this in two weeks, study these files and know your enemy!" Mr. Brown says.

That's weird Mr. Brown has just tipped his hat; he has never done that, boy oh boy, I believe there is something more than what he is letting us know. Let me ask the guys what they think.

"Ok, Goat Riders what do ya think, something feels different about this one?" I ask.

"Yeah, I think that you are on to something for once; there is something not right...his body language it's saying something." Dexter replies.

"Didn't I tell you Goon Snatchers, creepy, I'm gonna work on my tech and get it ready for this assignment. I suggest you two do the same. Sterling says.

We leave, but as usual, I'm happy as all get up for the assignment, never been to a national park, but I have been reading about the strange disappearances at them, and man it's been happening all over the country would love to solve this mystery. Even though Mr. Brown has not told us which park that we would be investigating, I'm still pretty hyped. Those lil weirdy kids have really got me thinking, so I yell to the fellas before they get too far ahead to hold on a second.

"Did you guys notice anything weird about those lil cave demons, you know outside of the obvious mess?" I ask.

"You mean besides those dead doll eyes and really pale skin?" Sterling replies.

"Well I did pick up on their energy aura in the videos; looks like they had snake hair right as the people let them get close and that weird white light energy from their eyes!" Dexter adds.

"Yeah, yeah, yeah all that good stuff, but who at our school did they remind you of?" I ask.

"Oh got it, you mean the Globsomes, well that's the name the kids at our old school are calling them just creepy they go to lunch and just sit together staring at their food, like it's gonna jump in their mouths or something!" Sterling says.

"Yeah you are right, even when I was the big bully on campus even I wouldn't mess with them; they just looked horrible. I got close and I could see blue veins pulsating through their nasty pale skin!" Dexter replies.

"Yep always wearing their hoodies, inside, outside, hot, cold that's our lead. When we get to Tubman middle school, we should investigate those Duck feet dudes!" I say.

We all agree and fist bump before we leave, and now we are pumped up and ready to go tomorrow it begins. This is gonna be good!

CHAPTER 2

Ok, so we are back at Tubman middle school; Sterling and I have been working on equipment that will detect if the Globsomes are what we are looking for. We've come up with some really cool stuff. Real hard to see, almost like little slick body cameras; just gotta give Dexter his equipment and we can do this.

"Hey you guy's ready to spy on the Globsomes, so ready to knock em right outta the school parking lot?" Dexter says.

"Yeah, but you might wanna check out our new tech, here are our communications devices; I made em based on designs by James West. So we can talk without being noticed!" Sterling replies.

"These little buttons, now these are really cool, testing, testing!" Dexter yells into the microphones.

"Hey man take it easy; that feed back is really loud; why do you always have to be jerk cake? Sterling says.

"Yeah dog cut it out, let's get the gear out. These little gems are attached to contact len's that are based on two inventors, well actually three Patricia Bath, Philip Emeagwali, and Mark Dean. Along with these cool watches, Ms. Baths invention helps treat cataracts; we have added the ability when you get up close to a person to scan their eyes for weirdness." I respond.

"We believe that the Onyx eyed kids are suffering from a mutated form of cataracts and other forms of creepy eye stuff, but this should detect it if any kid here at school has it!" Sterling says.

"Yeah, but can it detect eye snot, you know that stuff that is there when you don't wash your face right!" Dexter replies trying to be funny.

"Yep just like the stuff you have in your eyes right now, don't try to wipe it now. Let us continue; these watches use a one-gigahertz processor chip designed by Mark Dean and his crew, and Philip Emeagwali system that processes three-point one billion calculations per second. It will detect changes in body pressure and energy spikes, all ya gotta do is wave it in the direction of the one needed to be detected; if these guys are here, we got em. I say.

"Yeah, kinda of like the pressure that flies out of Dexter's butt after burrito day!" Sterling replies.

"Oh, that's right, I let one rip when you were in the library sleeping with your mouth open ooooooooh!" Dexter says

Two of us laugh really hard, you can guess which one doesn't. We gear up and start off to class when what do you know, here comes Turkeesha.

"So what are you bat tongued boys up too now?" Turkeesha asks.

"None of your business hamster hands, go count something!' I say.

"Good one, just because you say so don't mean that I'm not gonna keep my eyes on you Rat boys!" Turkeesha says

"Yeah, well I hope they fall out, nosey rosey!" I reply as I walk away.

I have class with one of the Globsomes, now to test my gear. My plan is to go to class and think on my feet; how do I get a monster to show itself without giving up my secret identity. Hmmm let me think, I got it.

Now that I'm in class, I will try to answer every question that the teacher gives, I may look like a nerd, but I gotta sacrifice for the name of science. When I go to the front of the class, I will scan with my watch for normal human body pressure and electromagnetic energy. And if you ain't human, this watch will tell on you quicker than a teacher's pet running to brown nose. It begins!

"Class, I will be asking questions about the short essays that you should have done last night along with other questions that will earn you extra credit. Let us start with the famous inventor essay, Tonya Perkins, you may go first." Ms. Peterson says.

Yeah, you creepy little sideshow I know that you are hiding something; I'm gonna just wait you out. Time passes a bit and most of the short essay questions have been answered, and it's my turn. I ask Sterling and Dexter, with our new communications gear if they are having any luck and no one is. I let them know that I'm gonna be the first one to catch a creepy. As I pass all the students on my way to the front of the class, I turn my watch in a way to scan each student as I pass them. I turn the ray scanner to infrared so they don't notice; man this equipment that we came up with is really nice. So I take my turn as Ms. Peterson calls on me to see what my report is about, Charles Henry Turner a native of Cincinnati, Ohio, Turner received a B.S. (1891) and M.S. (1892) from the University of Cincinnati and a Ph.D. (1907) from the University of Chicago. A noted authority on the behavior of insects, he was the first researcher to prove that insects can hear.

As I continue to give my presentation, I scan the class you know on the low, low. I'm actually getting some strange readings, but I won 't be sure until I walk down each aisle. I know I can walk down the isles while giving my presentation, now I can continue my work detective style. I can just wave my hands all around; the watch is set to vibrate mode. Now let me just wave my hand in that direction, bingo it is one of the Globsomes. WHOA, now that's creepy he seemed to notice me as my watch detected him. But that's all the truth I needed, now to finish this up and tell the other cats about this.

"Hey Dexter, Sterling you guy's reading me!" I ask.

"Yeah, I'm reading you loud and clear, hey how are you not getting in trouble talking in class?" Sterling asks.

"Oh I'm in one of the stalls in the bathroom, but the Gobsome that's in my class is one of em; he even seemed to notice the watch picking up his signal." I say.

"Well that's odd; they don't make a sound I made sure of it, guess it's time for me to check out my target. No word from Dexter yet you know how he is, over and out. Wait!" Sterling says.

"Why what's going on?" I ask.

"My watch is going crazy, I think I've got something the girl of the group she's looking right at me, man I get so nervous around girls!" Sterling says.

"Just play it cool, we can meet after this class, is done I'm out!" I reply.

I say that because I know that look that they give it is ghoulish, but now we meet up at our lockers seeing that class is over, we can report all of our Intel to Mr. Brown. Man Sterling really looks shook up, gotta talk to em calm him down.

"Man, I thought that she was gonna jump on me; her eyes went total dark on me. It felt like she was trying to steal my soul!" Sterling says.

"I know what you mean; the blue veins in my guys face where pulsing and jumping I thought I was gonna have to put the smack down in class. Which would have done nothing but blow my cover, but at least we know who they are now!" I reply.

"Hey, look Dexter is getting surrounded by the whole group of Globsomes, we'd better get over there and help him!" Sterling says.

"You are so right, if they fight one, they fight us all!" I add.

We meet up with Dexter at his locker and they seem to want to do him some serious hurt. They are giving off some weird energy and it's making my head hurt a little.

"So you bums wanna dance with the Dexter, just let me get my bat then we can discuss this like adults, what do ya say?" Dexter says while reaching for his battle bat from his backpack.

I grab his arm and tell him not now; we can introduce them to knuckle sandwich lunch, but not the heavy artillery not just yet. Oh boy the three of them stand side by side and we do the same when the principal comes in to get us straight, aw man.

"Is there a problem here, or would you six like to spend time in detention, Dexter you are no stranger to this line of questioning?" The principal asks with a raised eyebrow.

"But they started it; they came at me I'm not gonna run from these badger belly bums!" Dexter says.

"Sir, there's no problem we completely understand sir we're good; come on guys, it's lunch time. Sorry for the trouble!" I answer.

"Alright then, break this up and carry on." The principal replies.

"Man they are so lucky that the principal showed up!" Sterling says.

"Sterling, you need to quit that; you couldn't knock the shell off a Reece's Pieces, let's go to lunch where we can talk." I reply.

We get to the lunch room and take seats, the Globsomes come in and the chaos begins. It starts slowly then it explodes.

"Ok, so I just uploaded all of our findings to Mr. Brown he's gonna get back to us in a few." I say.

"Well I'm just itching to bust them up smelly mutants, running up on me like that; who do they think they are?" Dexter asks.

"YOU KNOW WHO WE ARE AND WE CAN'T LET YOU LIVE!" The three Globsomes say in unison.

We stand facing them and one of them grabs Dexter, that's when I smear cake from another kids plate in the eyes of the one that grabbed him. That's when it starts; you hear those famous words FOOD FIGHT. Everyone just starts going snow ape all over the place, food is flying, and Dexter punches one of the other ones. Then he gets thrown across the room into a really fat kid that breaks his fall. Then the adults come in and break it up. They take the Globsomes to the office because the cafeteria workers point out that they started it. Well what do ya know Sterling crawls out from under a table OMG?

"Well I didn't want to give up my secret identity, so I hid and acted like the normal me." Sterling explains.

"Guys I don't know about letting them go with the principal; this could be bad we should go check it out!" Dexter says.

"I'm way ahead of you, not only did I cake face that ghoulie, I stuck a mic-video tracker on him. The feed will go straight to Mr. Brown; two more classes then school will be out so then we can meet up with him. We did good today fellas, I'm gonna walk home and take all this in." I reply.

But hey check this out, after we left school the police were here everywhere, they are telling us that the principal is missing. Doing a lot of questioning of the staff, but me and the guy's know exactly what happened, the Globsomes. I'm sure Mr. Brown has it all by now.

Sterling and Dexter take the bus home. I want to walk and go by my favorite restaurant; exercise is good even at a young age plus the owner is good to talk with. My dad stresses this often, along with reading and finding answers on your own. The power of your mind has no rival, that's why I take the walk home gives me a chance to clear my head. The stuff that we see is pretty cool but intense; the sunlight is great easy to see how life thrives so well in it. My dad says never take the small things for granted, and I finally get it the world we live in is a smoke screen. The work we do has made that really clear; I read and research as much as I can that way, there will be no lie that can be told to me that I can't find the answer to. So now I'm here at the spot I guess I'll have the Chef salad, something light, before dinner because we did skip lunch.

"Mr. how are you today, I'm gonna try your Chef salad today just hold the bacon Blue cheese dressing please!" I say.

"So look at you trying to eat like an adult, well I guess you're never too young to learn proper eating for better health!" Owner.

"Yes sir, it will be the best like all your meals are!" I reply.

"You young man act very differently from most of the kids I see around here your age; ever since you won that video game tournament, you have made a real change. Not saying that you didn't always show signs of brilliance, it just seems something is different about you!" Owner says.

Well, the thing is, he doesn't know the half of it, if he only knew what I'm into now it would shock him, but then again, he seems to be sharp as well. He's always watching educational stuff, documentaries' Sasquatch type stuff like we hunt.

"Yes sir, been hitting the weights too, might be trying out for some school sports!" I reply.

"Good, a strong body and strong mind is great impressive how you've learned that you've got great parents!" Owner says.

"Like I always say, the best parents ever, but I have to ask a question have you been seeing any strange kids in the area?" I ask.

"Now that you mentioned it, these three little weird boogers came in the other day and scared the pants off me; it was like I turned around and there they were." Owner says.

"Wouldn't be two boy's and a girl would it!" I ask.

"Well, yes real pale strange eyes, they never said a word just moving through like ghosts. Used to be a dog that would hang out by the dumpster, that little joker took one look at those kids and yelped took off running and never looked back, haven't seen that dog since." Owner says.

"How long ago was that sir?" I ask.

"About two days ago, was just opening up for the day. Why do you ask?" Owner says.

" Well I believe news was talking about some kids that have been putting the fear in the adults around here. Looking for leads to give to the school news paper." I reply.

Of course, that's not what the real deal was, but I can't tell em what I really do now, can I. He raises an eyebrow like he knows something.

"Well hmm…here is your order hope you enjoy it, be careful on your way home!" Owner says.

"Thank you sir, I will but you make sure you do the same watch out for those little weird boogers." I reply.

I'll eat my salad on the way home, no matter how messy it will be; the Globsomes really get around, but didn't think that they would be causing this much trouble, hope the principal is found and ok. Great taste to the salad, bugs trying to get in it ok I'll close this up and eat it later, better step up the pace mom will be getting worried if I show up too late. The sunlight is great; it get's my melanin popping, wait I noticed that the Globsomes are always covering up their skin, hoodies, hats, sunglasses. I guess they burn in the sun like vampires that is very interesting, I'm gonna run that by Mr. Brown.

CHAPTER 3

Well just made it home and glad to see mom, she looks like she just got done weight lifting and now she's getting on the treadmill, I need to get in get my chores done, shouldn't take to long can't wait to see what Mr. Brown has for us tomorrow. Something about this case is a bit different. I guess we'll see later on, but time to hug my mother.

"Hey mom, I'm home!" I yell.

"I'm in the kitchen, did you eat?" Mom asks.

"Yes ma'am I got a nice salad on the way home, but I didn't finish it had a lot of stuff on my mind. We've got this new case with these weird dark eyed kids; they seem to have the agency confused." I respond.

"Mr. Brown as well?" Mom asks.

"Mr. Brown too mom. Is dad gone already?" I reply.

"Yes, he left about an hour ago; he finally got that old car of his running; when you get done with your chores, dinner will be waiting. Make sure to wash your hands!" Mom says.

"Yes ma'am that's a must germs and all; we got to see them up close and personal last week at the Lewis Latimer academy, the microscopes are really cool; see you're hitting the weights hard?" I reply.

"You know it a girl has got to keep up her fitness health, and girlish figure no matter what age you are, after awhile it's second nature; I love going to the doctor for check-ups and getting a clean bill of health!" Mom says.

She makes me proud with the way she takes care of herself; well I get the chores done; eat and watch a bit of TV. Then I feel the sandman knocking on my eyelids. So I kiss my mom good night and head to my room. I go to my laptop and connect with the fellas to compare notes.

"Guy's we've got a heck of a job ahead of us, so I guess that we need to double check our gear and new weapons." I say.

"I wonder where they are gonna send us; they didn't say which National Park it was supposed to be?" Dexter replies.

"That's a good question and you guy's are going to love the new weapons we've put together. Did they ever find the principal?" Sterling asks.

"I don't think so man; you know those freaks got em!" Dexter says.

"Well if they did, we have to find him as well as the other people missing; catch you cats tomorrow get some sleep you'r gonna need it I'm sure of it!" I say.

"Ok, I'm out." Dexter replies.

"Same here, wait did anybody notice when Sedale smeared that cake in the face of the weirdest one that grabbed you when he fell his pants fell down to exposing that pale veiny butt, I mean it had veins running all through it like a road map I almost hurled, just nasty?" Sterling asks.

"Dude only you would notice something that weird, but that would confirm they hate sunlight as if we needed more proof, I'm going to bed catch you cats later!" Dexter says.

I can't sleep now that I'm in my bed can't stop thinking about the world and all the troubles in it, glad it has us and we will make the difference. Let me set the alarm clock and read a bit. Always like to read under the blankets with a flashlight; for some reason helps me sleep and before I know it, I crash. I look at the toys that I used to love playing with when I was younger, that don't have the same value anymore the price you pay when you grow up, and the world is as different from make believe as fact...Or is it?

Oh man, I over slept again, got to get the shower and toothbrush going, face and hair washed. Ok, what am I forgetting oil my scalp that's right gives my hair sheen, nothing worse than a dry scalp I'm telling ya? Get my chapstick to keep my lips moist; cracked and bleeding lips are not a good look, I learned that from my dad. Ok last look into the mirror; I'm so fresh and so clean. Time for a quick breakfast; smells good my mom can cook. Still pressed for time though.

"Boy why are you in such a rush, sit down and enjoy your breakfast!" Mom says.

"I'm gonna be late for the trip mom. I can eat there I overslept." I reply.

"Um its 45 minutes before they come and pick you up. Are you feeling well. Don't you remember that you set your clock earlier now so that you don't over sleep?" Mom asks.

" I forgot, I can't believe that I rushed like that and didn't remember that I set my clock like that; thanks mom, I just got done talking with dad on the view chat he says he loves you and for me to be careful he always seems confident in me! I say.

We enjoy breakfast together; we talk about the trip and how I need to be careful. It's really good to be able to talk to my parents like this; both always have great advice and so much knowledge. What would I do without them; it's weird how she always looks out the window like a dazed stare when I'm about to leave. She's doing it right now, Mr. Brown always comes in and speaks quietly to my mother before we leave in a few minutes, and then we do it in style, each time the ride is different. But I'm ready to go; I hug mom then she kisses me, then Mr. Brown and myself leave.

"Are you ready for the information on the assignment, well this one is really a real tough case but as usual we are always close by but you won't see us?" Mr. Brown says.

"Yes sir, guess you're gonna wait till we pick up the other guys and get to the Latimer Academy?" I ask.

"Exactly, they've already been picked up and are enroute to the Academy we have additional small tech for your camping backpack trip. Trust me, you're gonna need it." Mr. Brown replies.

Now I just think about what is going to happen, but this case has got me a bit concerned, but I know that we've been training for this for quite some time. We pull up to the Academy and the fellas are getting out of their rides. They have the same blank look on their faces; you know, the one that you get when you are trying to figure something out.

"You bums ready?" Dexter asks.

"Yeah Pimple Pete, this might be the toughest one yet!" I reply.

"Well time to separate the men from the amoeba's, I need to get a drink at the water fountain; this water here is so much better than at the school." Sterling says.

"Ok, hurry up Thirsty Theodore we ain't got all day!" Dexter replies.

We get into the briefing room, and then we get all the juicy details for the assignment at hand.

"Well now that we are all here, I will explain to you the details of what your assignment will be. As you know, people have been going missing in the area, under strange circumstances. Because of the crafty work of Sedale, Sterling, and Dexter we now know what has been taking place. They are called Onyx Eyes, very strange and weird minions of a creature that has been plaguing the agency for a long, long time." Mr. Brown says.

He then energizes a screen so that we can see what they look like, without all the strange shadowy gear.

"They are also known as the melanin thieves, they take it because they can not produce it and from the one we captured, they have no pineal glands." Mr. Brown says.

"What is Melanin sir?" Turkeesha asks.

"Melanin is what all of us here on Earth have; it protects the skin from UV rays or sunlight. It helps regulates the thermogenic temperature found in most mammals, essential for maintaining metabolic balance within each cell like solar batteries." Mr. Brown replies.

"I thought you we smart you are such a fluke, everybody knows the answer to your dumb question!" I say to Turkeesha.

"Boy shut up; I always have a method to my madness!" Turkeesha says.

'The draw it from directly from the skin as you can see here in the footage, it is a very excruciating process. Notice how the eyes light up in that bizarre white light and their hair becomes like worms. Once they steal the Melanin, the person will burn from sunlight while their inner core temperature drops. If not returned in time, they will turn into a block of crystal ice literally. They are accountable for hundreds of missing people that dare venture into the national parks across the country, and your principal has become a victim and the Onyx eyes have escaped. We've tracked them to

Yosemite National Park, California, and that's where the four of you will be going. You will be pretend contest winners and will be accompanying some adults on an undercover nature hike. They have no idea of what is really happening, but of course, you have those pretend parents, so here are your new weapons and gear." Mr. Brown says.

Aw yeah dog this is the moment I was waiting for, the new gear!

"Sedale you have the new double wrist slingshot, and the ammo are these new exploding energy rocks with improved electronic tech that you have to mess with it a bit; you will be lightly surprised. Dexter, you have the basher bat equipped with three settings that will serve you well; check out the settings, one amplifies your striking power for starters. Sterling you have the potluck backpack it has everything you're going to need and more trust me, you will not be disappointed." Mr. Brown says.

"What about me sir, do I get any gear?" Turkeesha asks.

"Yes young ladywe'll supply you and explain what your weapons will do as well. We would never send you out in the field without proper gear." Mr. Brown replies.

These slingshots are the bomb they have little motors that fold up and down and even have targeted laser sight mounts, Dexter's new bat sounds like a light saber, Sterling must have some good stuff in his bag because he hasn't stopped smiling yet, I believe he's drooling.

"The briefing is over I don't have to tell you to be careful and watch each other's back out there. Bag the bullies, and we'll put them in detention for life!" Mr. Brown says as he leaves.

But then he stops and tells the three of us to come back, which is really unusual for him.

"You three have the scent on you and they know that you know who they are. I want to give you guys a few tips; they move around as well great distances with the power of small "Crystal Skulls." Mr. Brown says.

"You mean the same of one's of legend?" Sterling asks.

"The very one's and they are powerful; they actually aid in extracting the melanin from it's victims. Think of pouring water in a cup with a lid to close it and keeping it from spilling out; that's what these "Crystal Skulls" provide." Mr. Brown says.

"Man, so what are these weirdos exactly, seems like they know something we don't know sir?" Dexter asks.

"Well that's what you guys are going to find out, but they have been around at least during the time of Benjamin Banneker; he was a free African American almanac author, surveyor, naturalist and farmer, his timeline1731 to 1806 he made a slight mention of these creatures and actually fought them by tracking their behavioral patterns, based on the stars he was successful at stopping them, or at least the ones he encountered. History is a little vague on it or who assisted him." Mr. Brown replies.

"Well then sir I guess we have a really nice trip and a mystery to solve, we are up for the challenge!" I say.

"That's all I have; get to your flight Benjamin Banneker's patterns and charts are logged into your tech; you can pull it up or PDF it to automatically track them according to your settings. I recommend that you use that format to save time, now get out there and make it happen!" Mr. Brown replies.

He leaves and we take our gear and ready for the flight; he referred to the patterns of the stars, he didn't mention that Mr. Banneker was an Astronomer too, just thought I would point that out. We take our seats and take off with that whoosh; it is a smooth flight as usual what do you know Dexter is sleeping with French fries stuck to his face. So I start reading up on some scientific historical facts that are little known. So I come across this guy who started video games never heard of him but now I have; his name is Jerry Lawson, an engineer; I call out to Sterling to come take a look at what I just found out; he loves tech so he scurries over and I break the inventor down.

In 1970, he joined Fairchild Semi Conductors in San Francisco as an applications engineering consultant within their sales division. While there, he created the early arcade game *Demolition Derby* out of his garage. Our eyes light up and I continue. There, he led the development of the Fairchild Channel F console, released in 1976 and specifically designed to use swappable game cartridges. At the time, most game systems had the game programming stored on ROM storage soldered onto the game hardware, which could not be removed. Lawson and his team figured out how to move the ROM to a cartridge that could be inserted and removed from a console unit repeatedly and without electrically shocking the user. This would allow users to buy into a library of games, and provided a new revenue stream for the console manufacturers through sales of these games. Lawson's invention of the interchangeable cartridge was so novel that every cartridge he produced had to be approved by the Federal Commuincations Commission The Channel F was not a commercially successful product, but the cartridge approach was picked up by other console manufacturers, popularized with the Atari 2600 released in 1977. So there we have it the father of video games, Sterling goes back to what he was doing, but he seems more excited now with this new scientific info.

Sterling is now deep into his own newly issued tech making sure it works; as he's right on cue gets an electric zap, man that is so funny, but then I notice Turkeesha is looking at me. I look back at her and then she sticks her tongue out at me; what is wrong with her. Jeez she is annoying I'm too tired to eat so I take a nap; the trip is going to take at least five hours.

CHAPTER 4

Oh man, what a flight, I wake up just in time to see the park from above. So many trees covering what seems like a million miles in every direction I look; I bet if you get lost out here you are in a world of hurt. The mountains are huge and they seem to just unfold like pages in a book. The rest of the team is beating their heads against the windows, staring just as hard as I am, boy ya gotta love nature get out and enjoy as much as you can, but safely.

We land at a spot that looks like it could be an alternate base, but then we board a helicopter and go to the cabins.

"I wonder why we are taking a helicopter instead of just flying on the same plane?" Dexter says.

"Well if we did, it would probably mess up our cover." Sterling responds.

"Yeah, a super slick jet flying in and landing without an airport would really look crazy, remember low key." I say.

We land at the cabin, I get out and take a deep breath and now my chest is filled with pine scent, man the sky is nice and clear sunshine just makes me feel good to be alive, the birds overhead seem so free, well time to get a bunk in the cabin and meet the winners that will be our counselors, but they keep talking about this global warming thing how long will this last, with all these spooky things to deal with as well.

"Fellas, I have a new group name, drum roll please how about the "Battle Boyz." I say with my fists in the air!

They think over it for a few seconds, then they both smile and we all begin a group fist bump.

"Nice pop to it!" Dexter says

"Yeah it gives us a rough edge!" Sterling replies.

"Well I think it sounds stupid!" Turkeesha says.

"NO ONE ASKED YOU!" We all say at the same time.

We settle in after we have a healthy…Well I tried to eat healthy before turning in we meet the participants involved in taking us on the nature hike and campfire smoke screen, which we have to have to crack this case. We get to our bunks and have the prep talk before we go to sleep, but that tree line is really spooky though.

"That was some meal!" Dexter says.

"Dude you've never let a meal you didn't like!" Sterling replies.

"I can't argue that…wait oh yeah the meal your mom made now that was a first boiled Moose Nose; what was she thinking!" Dexter says.

"You guys are crazy, but that was a good one Dexter, what are ya thoughts on tomorrow?" I ask.

"It's strange even now I feel like we are being watched, now I know nothing can get in here with the security but checkout the tree line!" Sterling says.

"Man, it does have a weird vibe to it the sun is setting slowly it's like 8:55 at night!" Dexter adds.

"Don't look now, but is it me or did the sun really just drop? That ain't the worst of it check out the glowing white eyes in the tree line, a set of three!" I say.

"Well come on I'm ready to put knots on some pumpkin heads!" Dexter says clutching his bat.

"Yeah, you can't scare us!" Sterling adds looking intense and a lil worried.

I don't say anything just standing there tough you know, letting the guy's know I'm with em, but as crazy as the fast sunset an even crazier fog rolls in and it gets really quiet. I mean no noise or anything after we finish yelling out the window. Those almond-shaped white eyes don't go anywhere either, and lights out is called over the intercom. I can tell you as we climb in our beds, won't be getting a lot of sleep tonight one eye open and one eye closed!

So the next morning alarms go off, and we stagger out of our bunk beds; I feel pretty good, and now there is that weird feeling of something wrong again. We get the morning body cleaning routine going and notice that we are the only ones in the shower area. We get dressed and step to the cafeteria, then we start noticing there is no one anywhere on the campgrounds. Just wet floor signs I'm guessing from the night cleaning.

"Um where is everybody, there should at least be 13 guides here and kids?" Dexter asks.

"Oh, boy here we go; the creepy just got creepier from last night!" Sterling says as he pulls out his electronic tracker gear.

"So did you bug everybody like we planned yesterday?" I ask Sterling.

"Yep but there is a lot of interference, like a weird static charge it's messing with my tech!" Sterling replies as he slaps his gear.

"Let's start at the main office, should be some clues even if your wack gear doesn't show any." Dexter taunts.

"Wack?? Well better than just running around with a bat, barbarian boy!" Sterling replies he's always sensitive about his tech.

"You guys are too much; let's put our detective minds together and solve this mystery!" I say.

"Wait, wait my hat not the same without my Holmes hat!" Sterling replies running to his bunk to get his trademark hat.

"Really Sterling, that hat and shorts, now that's the weirdest clothing combination I've ever seen even for you man!" I say.

"Well somebody's gotta to win nerd of the year and this guy hasn't lost that since Kinder Garden!" Dexter replies.

"Ha, ha you guys are just soooo funny; let's go frog feet!" Sterling says as we leave and walk out the door through the building.

It's connected like one big section, I was thinking that it would be broken up into sections, you know kinda like school, but the way to the office is long and creepy things sure look different when there are no people around or in them. Smells funny in here like something was burning like a metal. You guys smell that I ask.

"You mean that brunt copper smell, yeah its coming from that room on the right, I think!" Dexter replies.

"For once you are right my scanner is picking up movement in that direction patterns are all over the place though?" Sterling says as he stops in his tracks.

"Hold up right here fellas let me try out one of my new Sling shot rocks, so ya saying that in the room on the left is where all the activity is? Let me peek in and get a quick head count!" I say as I stick my head in really fast and all of the Globsomes are surrounding and holding down one of the grown-ups.

I get my Reflecto Putty and my sling shot and fire it at the left corner wall, cool thing about this putty is it looks like mirror glass, and check this out it spreads on impact, but it makes almost no sound when it hits something, it sticks to almost anything. Now we can see what's going on without getting to close or even going into the room. Ya gotta love tech; ok now we are ready!

"Hey they look really nasty what are they trying to do to that guy, what's that wiggly thing they are trying to put on him!? "Dexter asks as he grips his bat tighter.

"It's some type of life form, maybe it helps them to take you without a fight, but there is one of those creepy crystal skulls floating in the air pulsating?" Sterling says as he holds his scanner up to get a better signal on what it could be.

"Well I tell you what fellas not on my watch, LET EM GO GLOBSOMES WE AIN'T IN SCHOOL NO MORE!" Dexter yells and smashes the creepy kid trying to put the lil monster on the counselor hard into the wall.

"Dexter aim for the skull, Sterling get ready to turn up the high-frequency signal; give em a head ache!" I say as we light the room up with our weapons.

We hit em hard and fast I fire my sling shots so fast that they don't have time to react, and Dexter is just going postal; he hits the grown so hard everybody is knocked off balance, and then Sterling pumps up the volume the Onyx eyed brats start grabbing their heads in pain, we got em, I believe we've got em on the ropes, when bam the eyes on the crystal skulls glow bright so bright we have to hold our eyes all except Sterling, his glasses automatically go into shade mode protecting his vision, gotta get some of those and just like that they all vanish...well try when I shot one of the bad guy's with my glue sling shot rocks, and Dexter hit's em so fast with his bat glowing full power, that he shatters the stink face all that's left is dust or I think it's dried skin, but the counselor is taken I mean just sucked into the skull and they vanish, so now we have to track em down, just add another one to the search and rescue list.

"Did we do it, did we stop em?" Sterling asks!"

"Nah, they got away and took the counselor with dang it!" Dexter replies.

"Let's get outside and find everybody, we can't wait; we may never find em all the power is out can't check the cameras!" I say.

We get outside and then Sterling has a pretty good fix on where the people are located. So we go out doors and notice that even though it's like 9 AM, it's getting dark and that tree line looks very spooky, but we gotta go get the people and stop the Globsomes.

"They are all in that direction it seems, can't nail it down 100% but that way is a good start!" Sterling says.

"We bagged one of the weirdos, and we collected that strange dust after we kicked it's butt!" Dexter replies.

"Well time to send a drone in ahead and try out the Pol-Go's, they are pretty fast powered by anti-gravity tech, we can cover a lot of ground with em!" I say.

"Been waiting to try these bad boys, yo Sterling trying not to fill ya diaper we know how much you hate heights." Dexter taunts.

"I not afraid Moose mouth; I'm just testing the wind for which direction it will be blowing so that I can move more effectively in the direction to cover more ground!" Sterling replies.

Well let me explain what a Pole Go is, remember the Po-Go stick well it's the same concept my friends, it's small like one of those old telescopes sailors used back in the day, once use have it you give it a good sling and it extends to like 4 feet long and about two inches thick. Handlebar extend and it even has foot mounts; you control which direction you go by pushin or pullin the handlebars right, left, front, or back speed changes with the handlebar grips, and hand breaks stop you. Now to get it started, you simply place your feet on the mounts and into the straps put ya helmet on and bounce like a Po-Go stick to activate the spring loaded anti-gravity engine, I know, I know so cool. We do it and we're off to find the missing people. Sterling was having a lil trouble but I think he's getting the hang of it now.

Remember Battle Boyz people have been coming up missing in this park for decades, and the park authorities have been trying to keep it quite; they want to keep the people coming, this place makes them a lot of money.

"Well the Onyx eyed kids are the cause no doubt!" Dexter replies we are talking through helmet mics to each other.

"That's means they've been doing this crap for a long time signal is saying that our trackers are in that direction; why does it keep getting darker it's so early?" Sterling says.

"Gotta be the skulls they are using, you know some weird magic!" Dexter replies as we zoom in and out of the trees.

It is an incredible ride, as we fly laughing and not focusing on the adult stuff we signed up for, we can see a world that we haven't seen much of and we need to keep places like this clear of the weird, the supernatural, and extra terrestrial. We get a signal below us, and we land to get to the bottom of this mystery even though I have a good idea what is causing this, we look around and notice that there is just a pile of clothing with no body, now we get serious like my father said always check your surroundings in an accident or crime scene.

"That's it, there is nothing left, no trace of the person that this stuff belongs to other than the tracker chip!" Dexter says.

"Yep, but it definitely belongs to one of our missing there are trace elements of human DNA in that direction but there is something else; you guys know what I mean!" Sterling replies and before he can finish, we are invaded. It's the Onxy eyed kids the last two and they break all of our Pole-Gos not to mention knocking us all over the place. And this gets the Battle Boyz really mad!

HENRY JOHNSON, NOW YOU SQUID EATING MUTANTS ARE GONNA GET IT! I yell.

"Yeah you leech lickers are gonna pay for that, ain't no principal gonna stop the butt whipping you pale freaks are gonna from us this time!" Dexter replies as he energizes his power bat.

"Oh yeah, yougonna know our butts chumps!" Sterling says as Dexter and I look at him slowly.

That's all you got, leave the comebacks to me or Dexter, please I say, they pounce and Dexter screams batter up and pops a fly ball hit on one of the mutants, the other one tries to take em to the ground but I chunk it in the head with my slingshot loaded with a shock rock, ZAP it goes skipping across the dirt holding its dome.

They come storming back kicking up a lot of dust; Sterling has made the sound that hurts their heads, into a beam that he fires from his phone. He begins to light them up as they keep trying to use the trees for cover, man do they look nasty and pale like they've been dumped in flour and mud. They keep trying lock eyes trying to peer into our souls I guess that's how they trap and getcha. Well, not today. Sterling has one on the ropes; she can't move as Dexter gives her a good smack with his bat and she stumbles forward then he finishes her off with a blast of Ultra violet light waves with one of his tech apps!

"OMG, SHUT HER UP SHE'S SCREAMING IS SHAKING MY TEETH LOSE!" Dexter yells.

Man he is not joking, but then she explodes not like the other one though we gotta be careful can't beat em all until we find the people; even though we have a tracker on em, we might need them to get some truth as to what has happened to all the other people over the years, I'm sure they have something to do with it.

"We got em two down one to go, this place has a really scary history people come up missing all the time in this national park, but nobody is investigating the area?" Dexter asks.

"Well actually they are, the government is involved or at least they know about it they are more concerned with money being made than the lives of the people!" I reply.

"Yeah they are afraid, but don't mind losing the people, so glad we have our organization to stop it according to my research here, this place is supposed to be full of aliens and monsters that are taking the people!" Sterling says.

"Dude grown ups they do really strange stuff sometimes, I wonder where the last one went, his butt has ball game scheduled with my bat?" Dexter replies.

He walks out from under the tree, and something is dripping on his shoulder, like a nasty luggie, but a bunch of it.

"Ewwww man, this is gross; what is this snot!" Dexter says and before we can answer he is yanked up into the trees.

"YAAAAAAAAAAH HEEELLLLLP FELLAS!" Dexter yells as he is carried really fast by the globsome but not before it wraps him up like a spider and smiles at us all in one quick flash.

He's gone; the only thing left behind is Dexter's Battle Bat, DEXTER WE YELL!

"YOU BRING HIM BACK RIGHT NOW, I'M GONNA MAKE YOU PAY FOR THAT SEDALE WHAT ARE WE GONNA DO?" Sterling asks trying to fight his tears back.

"Just hang tight bro, we will get him back and all the others they took I promise they are gonna pay for this!" I reply.

CHAPTER 5

My dad said, always have a plan and a backup plan, we are outnumbered and we think we know where the rest are. So we set up a drone to give us a better picture by adding the beeping signal of the trackers assigned to each person at the camp site. It goes up really high glad I brought it with us, it'll cut the time in half finding everybody. Sterling seems really rattled; I believe he's crying but trying to hide it.

"You good" I ask?

"Yeah I'm perfectly fine; I just didn't think they could get the drop on us like that. Especially big mouthed Dexter, I always knew he'd get his Bull Butt into trouble sooner or later!" Sterling says while trying to wipe his face without me seeing him.

"If I didn't know any better, I'd say you were crying for our friend?" I reply jokingly.

"Pff, if you think I care about that dog nosed jerk after all the beat downs he's given me over the years ya gotta be crazy; my frustration is for the others that never saw this coming, wait I have a signal and a visual of there location about half a mile in that direction!" Sterling says excitedly.

"Good well let's go find our people and get even!" I reply.

We walk as softly and quietly as we can in through the wooded trail, not that you can be totally quiet, so many leaves and trees, cool how the light beams break through the top of em, but it's still getting dark pretty quick, gotta be careful don't want to get ambushed again they move pretty quick before they attack. Suddenly we hear quick movements around us and in the trees.

"It's the Onyx's I just know it." Sterling whispers but is very focused.

"You ready?" I ask, and he nods his head yes.

"What are you two cabbage heads so tense for, it's just me?" Turkeesha says popping out of nowhere.

"Well, well if it isn't the Cootie Queen what are you doing here?" I reply.

"She's not so bad, I guess?" Sterling says trying to score points.

"Well ya dropped this power bat which is pretty cool!"Turkeesha replies.

"Quiet you two, there is something here get ready!" I say getting ready.

From what I can see, they attack by acting like innocent kids, and if they can they will drag you off to do whatever it is they do to you, but if they want a quick escape, they just use those creepy crystal skulls to suck you in then they're gone in a flash. I think you have to be in direct line of sight for them to use the skulls on ya; my dad always said pay attention to your surroundings and study potential threats well this one is a big one, seems different than the MoJa was, might be because there is more ground to cover in this forest.

"How did you find us?" I ask.

"I followed the cookie crumbs; you guys' love to eat junk food!" Turkeesha replies.

"Good thing Dexter doesn't stick to a strict diet even though we tracked em, he was still on point enough to leave a trail just in case tech failure!" I say.

"That's one of the first things we learned in class, never rely on anything totally!" Sterling relpies.

Outta nowhere, Sterling is hit with a snot-like goo that covers his back and pulls him back hard against a tree knocking the wind outta him. I jump and roll I take aim with my sling and POW, I knock big bug eyed creep outta of the tree by breaking the branch the creepy creep was standing on. As he falls, Turkeesha screams "He's about to be outta here" and turns Dexter's bat to full power and smacks em before he can touch the ground, far into the woods breaking branches on the way; I think I saw em skip off a big rock or two.

"WHOA DID YOU SEE THAT BISON BUTT SKIP OFF THE PLANET?" Turkeesha yells.

It was a clean hit; Sterling gives me a low microwave device that breaks down the weird goo that's got em stuck. He's free and doesn't thank me but the Cootie girl gets the thanks, that's when I turn my attention to the creep we're fighting I know he's coming back, and just like that we can hear him moving in the wood line but why does it sound like he's not alone?

"Oh you want some more...Well I got plenty for ya come on and get it then? Turkeesha says.

"Yeah stop hiding, Chitterling cheeks!" Sterling adds trying to sound tough.

I gotta tell ya something just doesn't feel right; before we can move it's behind Sterling and he's paralyzed and the mutant places the crystal skull on his back and he is sucked into it, and shot into the tree line, ya know in a beam of light, something seems to catch him. Well that's all I can stand gotta take em down and free my friends and the rest.

He moves really fast as he's right behind Turkeesha, so fast she can't respond. Oh man he's gonna do the same thing he just did to Sterling, not this hour I pull out my "Power putty" it's like C-4 when it hits and sticks it packs a power punch. I nail the chump right between the eyes, I yell to Turkeesha to drop and cover her head and BOOM! The mutant is blown to bits, she get's up pretty quick and starts bragging when outta of high trees falls a big monster, it grabs her and as quick as that booger cookie touches the ground, it takes her right back into the trees and outta sight, I have to track it, it's still moving in the direction of the others signals. Boy, oh boy it's almost completely dark now, need to activate my heat sensing glasses, it gives an image of anything that puts off heat.

Not much movement just weird colors, but they are pretty cool though I have to be really careful this thing strikes without warning. It gets really thick then it comes to an opening with a lot of strange crystal statue looking things almost like...Wait a minute, let me take the glasses off, this area of the woods look old very old, and these look like humans that have been trapped for a very long time vines are growing all over them, they look like the same stuff those crazy skulls are made of. I see our people, them all of em, around that round stone circle but none of them are moving; looks like they are gonna be sacrificed or something. I slowly sneak closer to get a better look, and they all are very pale, wait the statues are like a pale grey as well, man this is getting really strange.

I hear a sizzling noise and then WHOOSH the center of the stone circle is lit up in a huge Bonfire, it almost burns the arm hairs right off me, I roll really close to the other side I didn't realize that it had a huge drop off a cliff like a million feet down. I get myself together and stand with my back to the Bonfire, big mistake because I hear creaking and cracking from behind me, as I slowly turn I can see this nasty bug-eyed thing lower it's self from a tree, it's skin looks all wet and it doesn't look too happy to see me, it's the creepy cat that took Turkeesha and it has just thrown her to the circle, not in the fire but like it was gonna use her like the rest. This thing is at least 8 to 10 feet tall, long skinny arms and legs, long torso no ears or a mouth, ok scratch that mouth thing where there wasn't a mouth on the face a line is forming, teeth begin to show, this joker is smiling at me and goes down to all fours.

You're gonna turn everybody back to the way they were do you hear me, I try to say in my best tough guy voice, pointing my sling shot with "Shock Rocks" at the monsters face, it starts to circle left and right doing, seems like it's trying to jump me, I'm too close to the edge of the cliff need to get away from it, I keep hearing my dad's voice always be mindful of your surroundings, dad is really smart and tough so I respect his lessons. It jumps really quick and I fire my "Shock Rocks", quicker hitting it in the body electricity lights his butt up, I roll forward and out of the way of it and the cliff basically we trade places, it only smiles at me while covered in the electricity of my rocks.

Oh you think that's Ha, ha well try my "Mustard Marbles," these bad boy's burn like Mustard gas concentrated only hurting what they hit, no use holding back I'm not sure what's gonna stop this thing got to get it away from the people, it's not smiling anymore I don't think it likes the mustard marbles, it's shaking its head hard back and forth and into the dirt and leaves trying to get it off I think. It screams loud, then it looks at me angry and then it charges me, I run towards the woods and switch my glasses to night vision, it's crushing trees and everything coming in after me, I push branches and brush outta my way trying to put distance between us. Still, it grabs my leg and I pop it right between the eyes with one of my

"Flash rocks" to blind it. It lets me go but not before snatching my sling shot and crushing it, boy am I in trouble now, I've figured it out it's not getting darker this thing just puts like a dark force field over an area, they can't stand sunlight that's why they are stealing melanin so they can move around in the sun and do whatever it is they do, light is their weakness especially ultra violet light, you know sunlight it's still having a hard time adjusting to my last hit.

I need another weapon, and it's really fast "Oh snap," it just hit me, my rotating wrist sling shots; they shoot just as fast as a machine gun, with an insane amount of ammo plus I have my "Gyro shoes," that defy gravity and speed now let's try this again this is what I was trained to do. So now I have a plan I will run it through the narrow path, it's got loose rocks, and dirt all over the place, then I can light em up, so here goes I shout to it activate my shoes and get moving. This wet looking thing is fast I bounce from wall to wall keeping it off balance, then I come up on a small cave on the left, it's throwing fireballs at me blue and red everything around me is exploding. I fire three smoke bombs from my wrist sling shots to cover my tracks. These bad boys are the greatest, I didn't even realize that they work on nano tech that makes whatever type of ammo that you can think of, and what's even cooler is that it's linked to your brain waves harmless and safe, and it places like a video targeting system right in front of your eyes. So I have got to practice more with em, I won't trade in my sling shots though can't always rely on technology. I'm under cover now I can see em , he's crawling all over the wall like a big nasty ant, I notice that he has two glowing arms each one the color of the fire balls it was tossing at me, it looks like some giant version of the Onyx eyed kids I bet this is the king, a king mutant?

There are trees just in front of it; if I can push em in that direction then I got em. So I tear a piece of my sleeve off and attach it to a dart, and fire it dead on the hanging cliff tree, good it's taking the bait it's crawling to it just a little more now it's on the tree and smelling my sleeve and the air, so I yell to keep it there, "Hey you Slithering Sea donkey!" It looks and then I fire laser rounds and hit the rocks right above it's head and like in slow motion, the whole cliff crumbles down forcing the monster and tree down in a landslide burying it. I wait for the dust to settle I get a lil closer and there are still small rocks coming down, so I do what any kid does I find a branch and start poking the only part of the monster sticking out it's sickening wack arm. Good it's not moving I think its finished, I hit my pick up signal letting them know the mission is over and my location. Now I run as fast as I can to the spot where everyone else was left knocked out, and just like that my foot is hit with a white fire ball and I go flipping head over heels, it's not dead I can hear it crashing through the trees now I'm corned between the cliff and it, come on man now my wrist weapons are damaged.

It stands slobbering and bruised, it looks really angry so I guess this is it, wait what's that high pitch whistling sound like somebody dropped da bomb, with a heavy thud It's Mr. Brown landing right in front of me, man am I glad to see him. The creature speaks WOW!"YOU!?" it says. Mr. Brown stands in front of me and says I've got this, I'll take it from here you did great kid but this thing means to kill you, but I've got that thang for it.

The towering monster rushes Mr. Brown only to have Mr. Brown catch em with a solid jaw busting blow staggering it. It grabs Mr. Brown with those glowing arms and they start to light up, Mr. Brown places both hands on the creatures arms and tears one of them off, he then body slams the monster and like lightening he pulls from each side of his trench coat these devices that stick to the creature causing a high pitched sound and waves of ultra violet light the monster tries to grab its arm and run. Still, Mr. Brown stomp his foot on the arm telling the creature, Nah old friend this belongs to me, the monster darts faster than I could follow into the woods and vanishes. Mr. Brown was so fast and strong I just thought he was all talk; he just proved me wrong!

I couldn't stop it sir it was too strong, never seen anything like it, it seemed to have an answer for everything I thought of! I say.

"It was one of the most powerful entities on the planet; seemed pretty weak though, I've been battling this thing for quite awhile now; there are two others that are equally as dangerous. You did well considering and it only gets tougher as you go, now let's get our friends together and I will fill you in later about what you just faced." Mr. Brown replies in a calm voice like he's done this a million times.

He raises his hand with a smaller crystal skull, energy fires from it striking the giant crystal skull that was holding everybody in place and draining the Melanin from them, it shatters then sucks instead of blowing outward, well it does for a split second then quickly pulls into a light spiral then a loud pop. Everyone begins to wake, but none of them can talk; they can barely move; 8th line down, today was our toughest fight to date with the weird and the creepy. Mr. Brown seems more mysterious than ever as he orders the clean up crew and medics to tend to everybody. See we almost didn't make it I have more physical training and book studying to do if I'm gonna lead our team "The Battle Boys," this can't happen again because my name is Sedale, Sedale Jackson and our adventures are just beginning.

Unknown to Sedale Mr. Brown is having a conversation with a figure that was posing as one of the search and rescue staff; the figure walks to Mr. Brown but never turns and faces him directly.

"Does he know?" The figure asks, removing dust off pants with gloves.

"He's becoming a fine addition, better than I would have thought possible." Mr. Brown replies.

"DOES HE KNOW!" The figure asks again this time tilting his head over his shoulder with his back turned but a bit more agitated.

"No, but a kid that smart will eventually figure it out?" Mr. Brown says.

CPSIA information can be obtained
at www.ICGtesting.com
Printed in the USA
BVHW080010170921
616898BV00013B/911